Who Is the Beast?

BY KEITH BAKER

Voyager Books
Harcourt Brace & Company
SAN DIEGO NEW YORK LONDON

Requests for permission to make copies of any part of the work should be mailed to:
Permissions Department,
Harcourt Brace & Company,
6277 Sea Harbor Drive,
Orlando, Florida 32887-6777.

Library of Congress Cataloging-in-Publication Data
Baker, Keith, 1953–
Who is the beast?/written and illustrated by Keith Baker.
p. cm.
Summary: When a tiger suspects he is the beast the jungle animals are fleeing from, he returns to them and points out their similarities.
ISBN 0-15-296057-0
ISBN 0-15-200122-0 (pbk.)
[1. Tigers—Fiction. 2. Jungle animals—Fiction. 3. Stories in rhyme.] I. Title.
PZ8.3.B175Wh 1990
[E]—dc20 89-29365

First edition
E F G H I C D E F G (pbk.)

Printed in Singapore

The beast, the beast! We must fly by!

We see his tail swing low and high.

The beast, the beast! I must turn back.

I see his stripes, yellow and black.

The beast, the beast! I buzz along.

I see his legs, sure and strong.

The beast, the beast! Don't make a sound.

I see his eyes, green and round.

The beast, the beast! I hide from sight.

I see his whiskers, long and white.

The beast, the beast! I'm filled with fear.

I see his tracks — the beast is near!

Who is the beast? Who can it be?

I see no beast. I just see me.

Am I the beast? Could the beast be me?

I must go back to them and see.

I see whiskers, long and white.

We both have whiskers left and right.

I see eyes, green and round.

We both have eyes to look around.

I see legs, sure and strong.

We both can jump far and long.

I see stripes, yellow and black.

We both have stripes across our backs.

I see a tail swing low and high.

Both our tails swing side to side.

Who is the beast? Now I see.

We all are beasts — you and me.

The illustrations in this book were done
in Liquitex acrylics on illustration board.

The display type was set in Floreal Haas Bold.

The text type was set in Palatino.

Composition by Thompson Type, San Diego, California

Color separations were made by Bright Arts, Ltd., Singapore.

Printed and bound by Tien Wah Press, Singapore

This book was printed with soya-based inks on Leykam recycled paper,
which contains more than 20 percent postconsumer waste and has a
total recycled content of at least 50 percent.

Production supervision by Warren Wallerstein and Michele Green

Designed by Michael Farmer